Hodder Toddler

This book belongs to:

To Sue, who always cares.

SNUGGLE NUZZLES
by Jan Barger
British Library Cataloguing in Publication Data
A catalogue record of this book is available from the British Library.

ISBN 0 340 85549 5 (PB)

Copyright © Jan Barger 2002

The right of Jan Barger to be identified as the author and illustrator
of this Work has been asserted by her in accordance with
the Copyright, Designs and Patents Act 1988.

First edition published 2002
10 9 8 7 6 5 4 3 2 1

Published by Hodder Children's Books
a division of Hodder Headline Limited
338 Euston Road London NW1 3BH

Printed in Hong Kong

Snuggle Nuzzles

Jan Barger

Hodder
Children's
Books

A division of Hodder Headline Limited

'Got to go,' said Mummy, giving
Little Sheep a snuggle nuzzle.

'Got to go?' said Little Sheep.
'Can I go too?'

'Not this time,' said Mummy.
'Our friends will take care
of you until I come back.'

'Who will give me snuggle nuzzles while you're gone?' said Little Sheep. He loved Mummy's snuggle nuzzles.

'I'll give you squishy piggy squeezes,' said Big Pig. 'Will that do? Little Pig loves squishy piggy squeezes.'

'Squishy piggy squeezes are nice,' thought Little Sheep, 'but they're not snuggle nuzzles. I'll go and play with Little Cow.'

Little Sheep and Little Cow watched fish swimming in the pond.

'Mummy says wish on a fish,' said Little Sheep. 'I wish Mummy would come back.'

'Your Mummy will be back soon,' said Mummy Cow. 'Here's a mooey moo-cow cuddle. Little Cow loves mooey moo-cow cuddles.'

'Mooey moo-cow cuddles are nice,'
thought Little Sheep, 'and so are squishy
piggy squeezes. But they're not
snuggle nuzzles. I'll go and play with
Little Horse.'

Little Sheep and Little Horse raced across the field.

'Mummy says I run like the wind,' said
Little Sheep. 'I want Mummy to be here.'

'She's right,' said Mummy Horse.
'You do run like the wind. Here's
a snorty horsey huddle. Little Horse
loves snorty horsey huddles.'

'Snorty horsey huddles are nice,'
thought Little Sheep, 'and so are mooey
moo-cow cuddles and squishy piggy
squeezes. But they're not snuggle nuzzles.
I'll go and play with Little Goose.'

Little Sheep and Little Goose chased Big Goose. Big Goose let Little Sheep catch her.

'I can catch my Mummy,' said Little Sheep,
'when she doesn't have to go away.'

'You'll catch her again soon,'
said Big Goose. 'Here's a beaky
goosey peck. Little Goose loves beaky
goosey pecks.'

'Beaky goosey pecks are nice,'
thought Little Sheep, 'and so are snorty
horsey huddles, mooey moo-cow cuddles
and squishy piggy squeezes. But they're
not snuggle nuzzles. I'll go and play with
Little Dog.'

Little Sheep and Little Dog rolled
in the grass. 'Don't get dirty!'
said Mummy Dog.

'Mummy says that, too,' said Little Sheep.
'But she's not here.'

'Your Mummy won't be gone long,' said Mummy Dog. 'Here's a sniffy doggy snuffle. Little Dog loves sniffy doggy snuffles.'

'Sniffy doggy snuffles are nice,'
thought Little Sheep, 'and so are beaky
goosey pecks, snorty horsey huddles,
mooey moo-cow cuddles and squishy
piggy squeezes. But they're not
snuggle nuzzles.'

When Mummy came back she gave Little Sheep an extra special, snugglier than ever, long lovely snuggle nuzzle.

'My friends give me sniffy doggy snuffles, beaky goosey pecks, snorty horsey huddles, mooey moo-cow cuddles and squishy piggy squeezes,' said Little Sheep.

'But Mummy's snuggle nuzzles
are the best of all!'

Goodbye
Hodder Toddler